Flower Girl
Butterflies

SCHOLASTIC INC.

New York Toronto London Auckland Sydney
Mexico City New Delhi Hong Kong Buenos Aires

Flower Girl Butterflies

By Elizabeth Fitzgerald Howard

Illustrated by Christiane Krömer

Something Special

Aunt Robin is getting married!
She is going to marry somebody nice called Jeff.
He will be my new uncle—Uncle Jeff.
I have never been to a wedding,
but Aunt Robin wants me to be her flower girl.
Flower girls are supposed to walk down the aisle
in front of the bride and scatter flowers from a basket.
Everybody will be watching me.

I know I'm going to be scared.

A New Dress

Soon after Aunt Robin asked me to be her flower girl,
she said, "Sarah, we have to go shopping!
We must buy you a pretty dress to wear in my wedding."
So we went downtown to a store that sells flower girl dresses.

I tried on five pretty dresses.
The fifth one was the best.
When I twirled in it, the skirt flew out all around me.
"What do you think, Sarah?" Aunt Robin asked me.
"Which one do you like?" I asked Aunt Robin.

"The one you have on now," she said, giving me a hug.
"Ooooh, Aunt Robin," I said.
I just knew my aunt and I would choose the same dress.
I love my beautiful dress so much!
But I'm still scared about being a flower girl.

Butterflies

Aunt Robin says I have to walk
from the way, way back of the church
to the way, way front
and stand beside her for the whole wedding.
But suppose I forget to throw the flowers?
Suppose I drop my basket?
Suppose I trip and fall down?
Maybe something will happen
so I can't be a flower girl.
Maybe I will get a sore throat.
And measles. And chicken pox, too.
I can't be in the wedding if I'm sick.

Maybe Snuffy and Spoofy will steal
my new white party shoes and chew holes in them,
the way they chewed Daddy's new sneakers.
I can't be a flower girl if my party shoes are all chewed.
Maybe the wind will blow my flower girl dress
out of the window into a mud puddle.
I can't walk down the aisle in a muddy dress.
I told Aunt Robin how I felt.
"Sarah," she said, "I will be so sad
if you are not my flower girl."
I don't want Aunt Robin to be sad.
But I don't like being scared. And I am.

Guests Are Coming

The wedding is tomorrow.
Some relatives will be staying at our house.
I helped Mommy think where everyone could sleep.
"My room will be a good place," I told Mommy.
I will sleep in the TV room
with my cousin Trina and my cousin Amy.
Aunt Susan and Aunt Laura will sleep in my room.
I made space on my desk for all their makeup and perfume.

My two grannies are going to sleep in our real guest room, where they will talk a lot. Cousin Chaz and Uncle Chucky and Uncle Joey will sleep in the attic. Uncle Joey always picks me up to ride on his shoulders. Uncle Chucky always has candy in his pockets, which he sneaks to me.

Cousin Chaz plays pretend games with me.
Today we pretend my house is a hotel.
"Room service!" Cousin Chaz calls.
I take him a banana and
a glass of milk on a tray.
I almost forget that I am scared
about the wedding.

The Rehearsal

We have to practice walking down the aisle.
It's about a mile long.
"My tummy feels funny," I whisper to Mommy.
"Oh, honey, it's just butterflies," says Mommy.
"Look, there is Uncle Jeff's little cousin, Willie.
Willie is the ring bearer.
He will carry the wedding rings on a pillow
just the way you will carry your basket of flowers."
But Willie is holding tight to his mom. I can tell he is very, very scared.
Oh, dear! Willie is lying on the floor.
Now he is crying and kicking his feet.
He says he won't be the ring bearer.
He says he won't even come to the wedding.
I look at Aunt Robin. She has tears in her eyes.
"Willie," I call to him, "Willie, watch me when I walk."
Willie stops crying and kicking.
He watches me. I wonder if he knows that I'm scared, too.

The Big Day

Today is the wedding!
What a busy morning!
The telephone and the doorbell never stop ringing.
Eleven packages come in the mail for Aunt Robin.
The man in the brown truck brings seven more.
People bring flowers. And flowers. And more flowers.
And my flower girl basket!

All the uncles and aunts and cousins and grannies
get dressed for the wedding.
"Sarah, can you thread my needle?" my short granny asks.
"Sarah, can you buckle my belt?" my tall granny says.

I put on my tights and party shoes
and then my beautiful flower girl dress.
I feel like a princess.
Then I remember the long walk
to the way, way front
of the church.

The Wedding

In the back of the church Aunt Robin smiles at me.
She looks like a fairy queen in her wedding dress.
"Sarah," she says, "you are so beautiful,
and I am so happy that you are my flower girl."
Aunt Laura is buttoning my last button.
Aunt Susan is fluffing up my sash.
I'm so excited!

I take a deep, deep breath.
I will not forget to throw
the flowers just right.
I will not drop my basket.
I will not trip and fall.
"You will be wonderful, Sarah,"
Mommy says. She kisses me
and goes to sit with Daddy.
When the music starts,
the bridesmaids walk
down the aisle, one by one.
There goes Willie!
He is carrying the little pillow
with the wedding rings
fastened on tight,
and he's not crying.
I smile at him.
It's almost my turn.
Now?

Now!

The Party

I did it!
And I forgot to be scared!
Willie didn't cry once.
Now we are all smiling at one another
and smiling for the photographer.
And eating.
And dancing.

Aunt Robin dances with Uncle Jeff.
Mommy dances with Daddy.
My grannies are dancing with my uncles.
Aunt Laura and Aunt Susan are dancing with everybody.
I am dancing with Cousin Chaz,
and my flower girl dress is twirling and twirling.
Willie and I try dancing together,
and we both fall down laughing.

After we eat delicious wedding cake,
Aunt Robin and Uncle Jeff
leave for their wedding trip.
We throw birdseed at them.
Now the wedding is over.
As I fall asleep, I think to myself,
I loved being the flower girl!
I wonder if Aunt Laura or Aunt Susan
will be getting married soon!

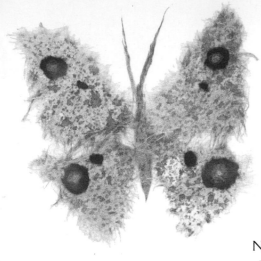

ISBN 0-439-70316-6

Text copyright © 2004 by Elizabeth Fitzgerald Howard. Illustrations copyright © 2004 by Christiane Krömer. All rights reserved. Published by Scholastic Inc., 557 Broadway, New York, NY 10012, by arrangement with Greenwillow Books, an imprint of HarperCollins Publishers. SCHOLASTIC and associated logos are trademarks and/or registered trademarks of Scholastic Inc.

12 11 10 9 8 7 6 5 4 3 2 1   5 6 7 8 9 10/0

Printed in the U.S.A.   40

First Scholastic printing, February 2005

Watercolor, colored pencils, and collage materials were used to prepare the full-color art.

The text type is Della Robbia.